AF594801

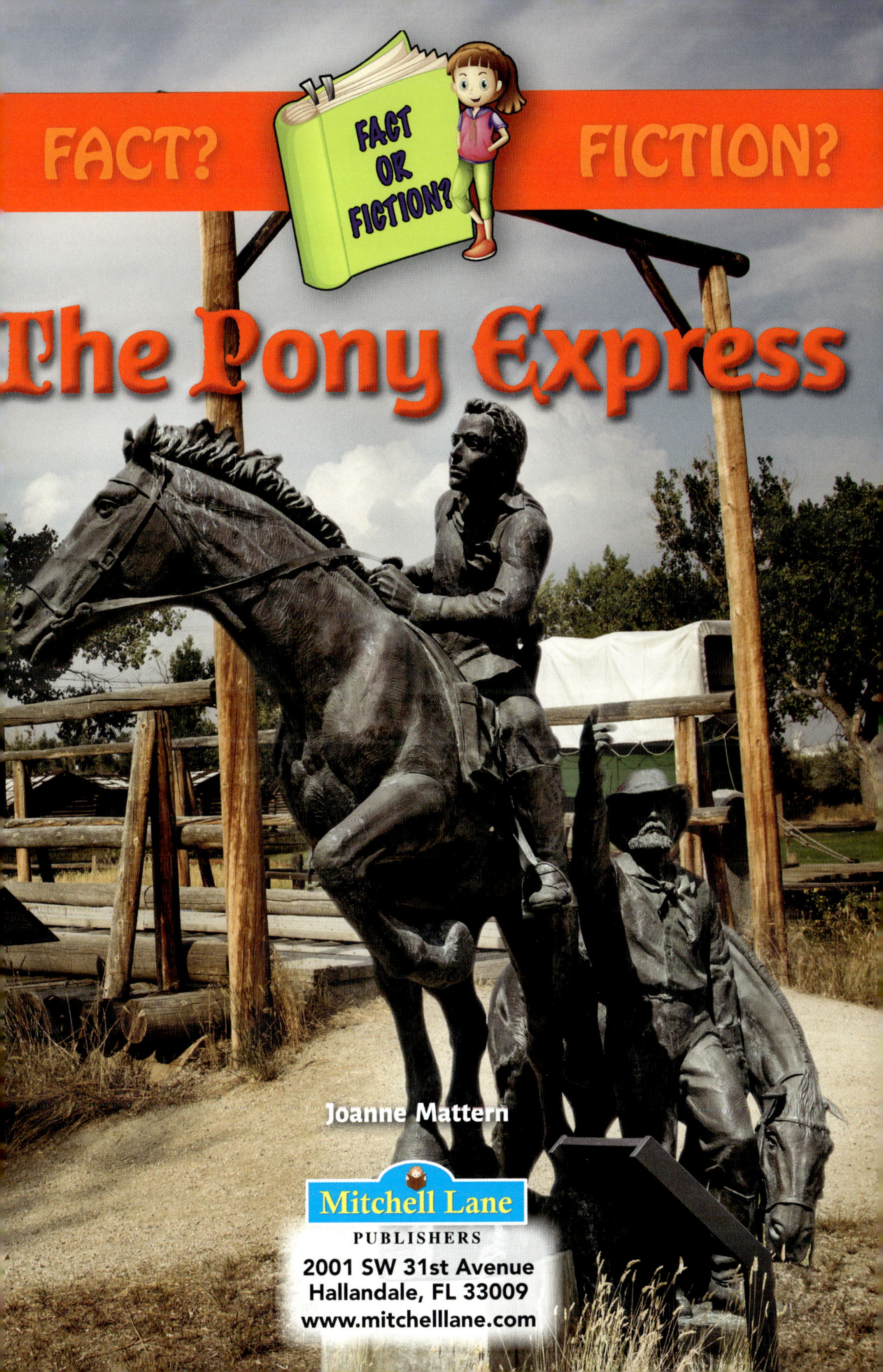

The Pony Express

Joanne Mattern

Mitchell Lane
PUBLISHERS
2001 SW 31st Avenue
Hallandale, FL 33009
www.mitchelllane.com

 Printed and bound in the United States of America.

Printing 1 2 3 4 5 6 7 8

Audie Murphy
Buffalo Bill Cody
The Buffalo Soldiers
Davy Crockett
Ethan Allen and the Green Mountain Boys
Eliot Ness
Francis Marion
The Pony Express
Robin Hood
The Tuskegee Airmen
Wyatt Earp
Zorro

Library of Congress Cataloging-in-Publication Data
Names: Mattern, Joanne, 1963– author.
Title: The pony express / by Joanne Mattern.
Description: Hallandale, FL : Mitchell Lane Publishers, [2018] | Audience: Age: 8-11. | Audience: Grade 4 to 6. | Includes bibliographical references and index.
Identifiers: LCCN 2017009131 | ISBN 9781612289649 (library bound)
Subjects: LCSH: Pony express—Juvenile literature.
Classification: LCC HE6375.P65 .M225 2017 | DDC 383/.1430973—dc23
LC record available at https://lccn.loc.gov/2017009131

eBook ISBN: 978-1-61228-965-6

CONTENTS

Words in **bold** throughout can be found in the Glossary.

"Pony Bob" Haslam, one of the Pony Express's most famous riders, is pictured in 1908. Forty-eight years earlier, he completed the longest round-trip ride in Pony Express history.

CHAPTER 1
The Longest Ride

Bob Haslam was waiting for the mail. The Pony Express rider was only 20 years old in May 1860, but he was already an experienced horseman nicknamed "Pony Bob." Haslam's job was to carry the mail from Friday's Station in the Nevada **Territory** to Bucklands Station, about 75 miles away. He knew the journey was dangerous, Even so, as he waited for the previous Pony Express rider to come in from the west, he had no idea of the adventure that was about to begin.

When the rider arrived, Haslam jumped into the saddle of his horse and galloped away. Because Pony Express riders traveled so hard and fast, they changed horses at stations every 10 to 15 miles along the route. But when Haslam reached Reed's Station, no fresh horse awaited him. Local settlers were engaged in a war with a Native American nation called the Paiute. They had taken all the horses to use in battle. Haslam had no choice but to force his tired mount to continue.

Haslam finally reached Bucklands. He could not wait to eat and rest. But no fresh rider stood waiting to take the mail. Puzzled, Haslam went inside. Johnny

Richardson, who was supposed to be the next rider, was playing cards with **station keeper** W.C. Marley.

Haslam asked what was going on. Marley told him that Richardson was so afraid of the Paiute that he refused to ride. The station keeper knew the mail had to go through. He offered Haslam 50 dollars, a large sum of money in those days, if he continued to the next station. Haslam replied, "I will go at once."[1] Ten minutes later, he was back on the trail.

It was more than 120 miles to the next stop at Smith's Creek. The journey took him across a sandy desert where clouds of harsh dust choked both Haslam and his horse. They traveled 30 miles without water until they reached a **relay station** at Sand Springs. Haslam changed horses and pushed ahead.

Signs at Sand Springs Pony Express Station, Nevada

Some stone walls are all that remain of the Sand Springs Pony Express Station in the middle of the Nevada desert.

When he reached the Cold Springs station, the station keeper offered to finish the run. Haslam refused. Mounting a fresh horse, he rode the rest of the way to Smith's Creek.

Haslam *still* wasn't done. After a few hours of sleep, it was time to get back to work. The rider who came in from the east had been injured. Could Haslam take the mail back west? He said yes.

Haslam galloped back over the route he had just completed, keeping an eye out for Paiute. The Native Americans had attacked Pony Express riders and tensions between the Native Americans and the company were getting worse every day.

Years later, Haslam recalled the frightening ride:

> It was growing dark, and my road lay through heavy sagebrush, high enough in some places to conceal a horse. I kept a bright lookout, and closely watched every motion of my poor pony's ears, which is a signal for danger in an Indian country. I was prepared for a fight, but the stillness of the night and the howling of the wolves and coyotes made cold chills run through me at times.[2]

When he arrived at Cold Springs, he found a terrible sight. The station had been burned to the ground. Even worse, the station keeper lay dead on the ground, his body full of Paiute arrows. Haslam could not leave Cold Springs fast enough. He rode through the night. He found out later that he had ridden right through a ring of Paiute traveling in the area. Somehow they did not spot the lone rider.[3]

Finally, Haslam reached Friday's Station. He was so exhausted that he had to be helped inside. Haslam had just completed the longest round trip in Pony Express history. He had traveled 380 miles in 36 hours with little rest and danger stalking him at every turn.[4]

Haslam was hailed as a hero for his actions and became one of the Pony Express's most famous

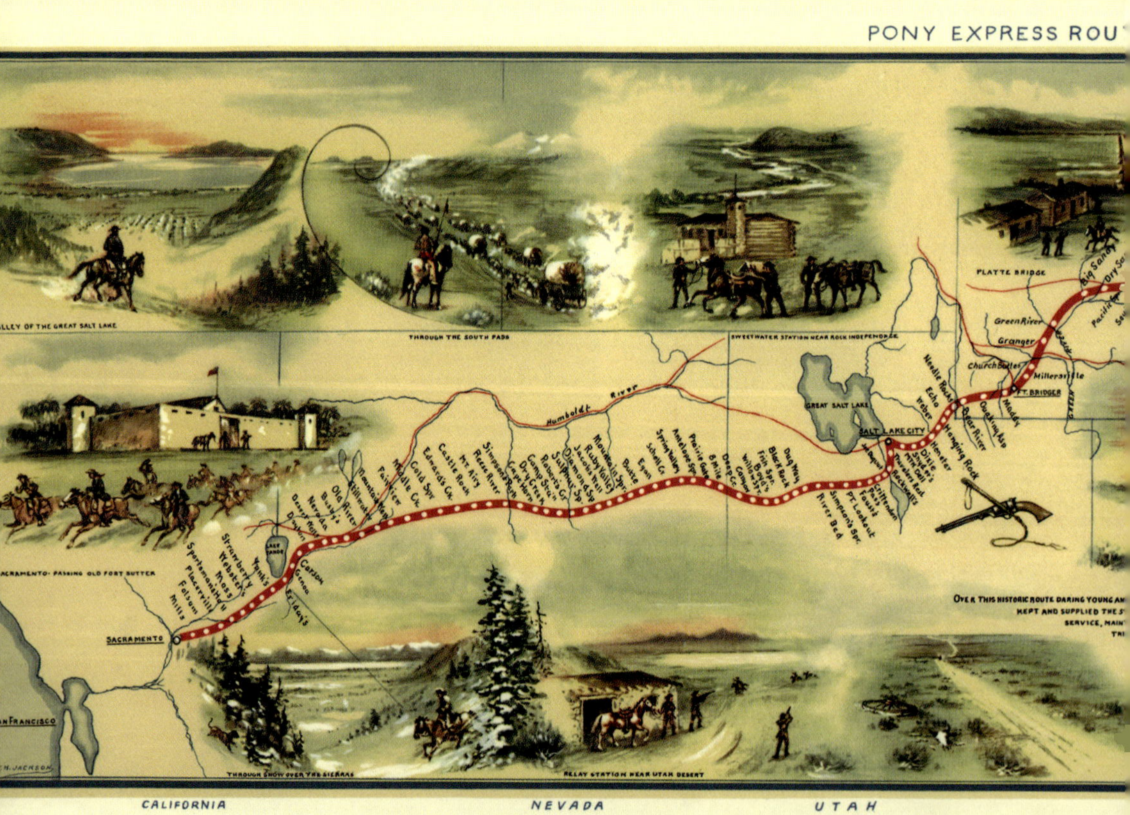

Noted Western landscape artist William Henry Jackson created this route map of the Pony Express in 1935. The 1900-mile (3100km)

riders. His adventures, and the deeds of other Pony Express riders, created an American legend. Today we still hear stories of these brave riders, who put themselves in danger every day just to deliver the mail. The Pony Express is an inspiring success story. Or is it? The fact is that the Pony Express was only in business a short time and lost a huge amount of money. However, it changed America. Read on to learn the legends and the facts about the quick rise and even faster fall of the Pony Express!

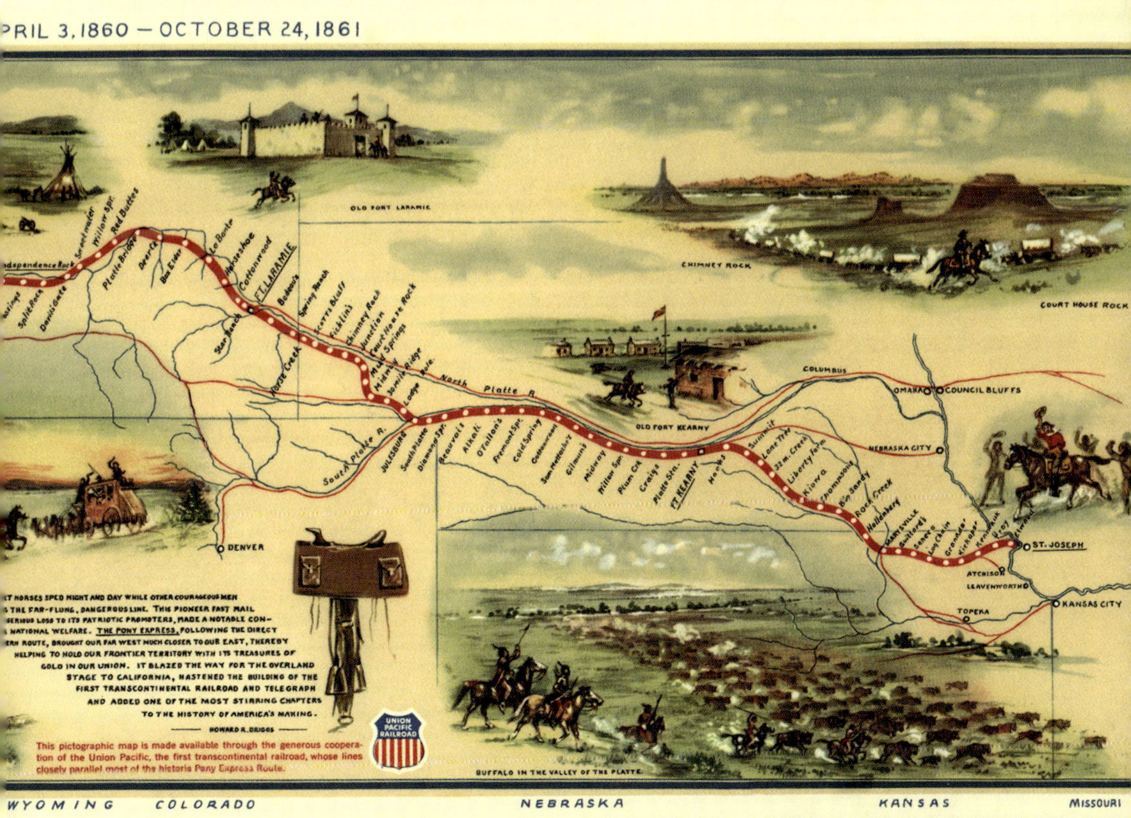

route followed many wagon trails, including the famous Oregon Trail, and crossed deserts, mountains, and rivers.

PONY EXPRESS!

CHANGE OF TIME!

REDUCED RATES!

10 Days to San Francisco!

LETTERS

WILL BE RECEIVED AT THE

OFFICE, 84 BROADWAY,

NEW YORK,

Up to 4 P. M. every TUESDAY,

AND

Up to $2\frac{1}{2}$ P. M. every SATURDAY,

Which will be forwarded to connect with the PONY EXPRESS leaving ST. JOSEPH, Missouri,

Every WEDNESDAY and SATURDAY at 11 P. M.

TELEGRAMS

Sent to Fort Kearney on the mornings of MONDAY and FRIDAY, will connect with **PONY** leaving St. Joseph, WEDNESDAYS and SATURDAYS.

EXPRESS CHARGES.

LETTERS weighing half ounce or under.............. $1 00

For every additional half ounce or fraction of an ounce 1 00

In all cases to be enclosed in 10 cent Government Stamped Envelopes,

And all Express **CHARGES** Pre-paid.

☞ **PONY EXPRESS ENVELOPES** For Sale at our Office.

WELLS, FARGO & CO., Ag'ts.

New York, July 1, 1861.

This poster, issued in July, 1861, emphasizes the speed of the Pony Express in delivering mail across the continent. It also reflects the reduction in rates from the original charge of $5 per half ounce.

CHAPTER 2

The Need for Speed

Today communication is easy and quick. We can call, text, or e-mail someone anywhere in the world and get a response in minutes or seconds. A package can travel across the country in a day.

Things were very different during the mid-1800s. Most people in the United States lived east of the Mississippi River. However, as the government made more land available in the West, increasing numbers of people traveled there and settled in new places far from home. Then, in 1848, gold was discovered in California. Thousands of people headed west to seek their fortune. These new settlers discovered that it was almost impossible to keep in touch with their family and friends back home. William Swain, who left his farm in New York to pan for gold in California, expressed a common feeling in a letter to his family, saying, "I cannot express the disappointment I have experienced in not as yet having received any letters."[1]

At that time there were few ways to deliver mail across the United States. Some wagon trains carried mail, but it could take five or six months to complete their trek. It was actually faster to send mail by ship.

However, because there was no direct water passage between the east and west coasts of the United States, ships had to travel nearly 8,000 miles around Cape Horn at the tip of South America to get from New York to San Francisco. Later, a railroad across the Central American country of Panama shortened the journey, but it still took more than a month for mail to reach the opposite side of the country.

In 1857, John Butterfield's Overland Mail Company received a government **contract** of $600,000 a year to transport mail.[2] Butterfield's route was called the Oxbow Route and covered 2,795 miles across Missouri, Tennessee, Arkansas, Texas, the territory that would become Arizona, and finally up to San Francisco. Butterfield's **stagecoaches** carried both passengers and mail and could cover the entire route in 25 days or less.[3] To do this, Butterfield stuck to a demanding schedule and warned his drivers that "Every person in the Company's employ will remember that each minute is of importance. If each driver on the route loses 15 minutes, it would make a total loss of time, on the entire route, of 25 hours, or, more than one day."[4]

Butterfield's company was a big step forward, but many people in the west felt there had to be a better way. They believed a route through the central part of the United States would be shorter and faster. Many suggested a service that followed the Oregon-California Trail, which brought pioneers and soldiers from Missouri to the West Coast.

In 1860, a businessman named William H. Russell decided to try something new. Along with his partners

William Waddell and Alexander Majors, Russell started a company called the Central Overland California & Pike's Peak Express Company, or the COC&PP Express. Russell announced that the company would run a private mail service carried entirely on horseback. Russell and his partners had earned their fortunes moving freight across the country and felt they had the experience necessary to move the mail in the same way. Author Arthur Chapman described Russell's dramatic plan: "Men and horses were to form a veritable **telegraph** line of flesh and blood between the muddy Missouri and the bright Pacific. It was to be a super-service of speed, kept going day and night at all seasons of the year."[5]

Russell did not waste any time. On January 27, 1860, he wrote to his son, "Have determined to establish a Pony Express to Sacramento, California, commencing 3rd of April."[6] He also noted that the mail would be delivered in 10 days, less than half the time of Butterfield's route. Russell and his partners had just two months to put their plan into action.

Travel across the West was dangerous. This stagecoach is guarded by soldiers riding on top of the wagon.

Pony Express rider Frank E. Webner is pictured on his horse in 1861. The photo clearly shows how young Webner was. Many riders were in their teens.

CHAPTER 3

The First Ride

Starting the Pony Express would be expensive. Russell and his partners spent $100,000 to get started. Russell believed that if he could make the Pony Express a success, he would win a government contract worth a lot of money to continue carrying the mail across the country.

The route stretched 1,966 miles between St. Joseph, Missouri, and Sacramento, California. It was divided into five divisions, each one managed by a division **superintendent**. **Home stations** were 75 miles apart. Relay stations lay about every 15 miles between the home stations so riders could change horses. The company bought the best horses they could find. They often spent up to $200 per horse, a very large sum of money at that time.

Along with people at all the stations and excellent horses, the Pony Express needed riders. Beginning in March 1860, newspapers along the route carried announcements like the one that appeared in the *Sacramento Daily Union*: "MEN WANTED! The undersigned wishes to hire ten or a dozen men, familiar with the management of horses . . . on the Overland Express Route via Salt Lake City.

Wages $50 per month."[1] Legend has it that another advertisement played up the danger of the new job: "Wanted—young, skinny, wiry fellows not over 18. Must be expert riders, willing to risk death daily. Orphans preferred."[2] Young men from all over the west responded enthusiastically, and filled the 80 available jobs in just a few days.

All these costs meant that the company had to charge a lot to mail a letter. A letter weighing just half an ounce cost $5.00. That would be at least $75 today. **Telegrams** cost about $3.50 for the first 10 words, and more for longer messages.

The Pony Express depended on speed, so riders couldn't weigh very much. They also had to use a lightweight mailbag. A special bag called a mochila was designed. Each mochila fit over the saddle and could be put on and taken off quickly when riders changed horses. The riders only had two minutes to do that. One time the transfer took just 11 seconds! A mochila had four mail pouches—two on each side. Each pouch was called a cantina and was locked with a special key. One of the cantinas held a timecard. It showed the times of arrival and departure at each station.

Newspapers carried enthusiastic articles about the new mail service. When it started on April 3, the cities of St. Joseph, Missouri, and Sacramento, California, were filled with excitement. In St. Joseph, crowds gathered in the streets in front of the train station. A band played and Mayor M. Jeff Thompson gave a speech. The restless crowd waited for a train carrying mail from New York City to arrive.

While no one is absolutely sure who the first Pony Express rider was, most historians say it was a young man named Johnny Fry. Fry waited impatiently along with the crowd. It surrounded the horse that would carry the mail. Unfortunately, the train was three hours late. People plucked so much hair out of the horse's tail to keep as souvenirs that Fry finally brought it back to the stable for safety.

Finally, the train puffed into the station. Fry loaded 49 letters, six telegrams, and special editions of East Coast newspapers into his mochila. A cannon boomed out a salute, and Fry and his horse galloped away. He rode 80 miles to Marysville, Kansas, where he turned his mochila over to the next rider. The *St. Joseph Weekly West* described the event as "The Missouri and Pacific United! The Greatest **Enterprise** of Modern Times!!"[3]

Ten days later, rider Bill Hamilton rode into Placerville, California, near Sacramento. He was greeted by bands playing, people cheering, and an escort by the mayor to Sacramento. The *Sacramento Union* exclaimed, "Hip, hip, hurrah for the Pony Carrier!"[4] A small steamer carried the mail down the Sacramento River to San Francisco.

At the same time, riders raced eastward from Sacramento to St. Joseph. As with the westward riders, the first carrier was sent off with a big celebration. Ten days later, after struggling through miles of bad weather, mud, and snow, the final rider delivered the mail to a cheering crowd in St. Joseph. The first runs of the Pony Express had been a huge success. But many challenges lay ahead.

William "Buffalo Bill" Cody was a Pony Express rider and the most famous showman of the American West. His Wild West Show brought tales of adventure to audiences all over North America and Europe.

CHAPTER 4

Danger on the Trail

The public loved the idea of the Pony Express. Many people thought of the riders as heroes, brave young men with a sense of adventure who would do whatever they had to in order to get the mail through to the next station. No doubt, these men loved the attention and enjoyed being called heroes. However, they worked very hard.

Pony Express riders spent hours in the saddle. They had to know how to handle high-spirited horses that could easily throw or injure them. They had to deal with extreme weather and natural disasters, such as heavy rain, mudslides, blizzards, hailstorms, floods, and fires. They traveled through burning hot deserts and snow-covered mountains. In addition, there was the ever-present danger of attacks by Native Americans or **outlaws** looking to steal valuables from the mail.

Several Pony Express riders became famous. One of the most colorful was William F. Cody, later known as Buffalo Bill. Cody was only 14 when he joined the Pony Express, but the young man soon got a reputation for being fearless. Stories often had him outwitting outlaws and facing other dangers. In one famous tale (which may or may not be true), Cody had to carry a large sum of money through an area filled with bandits. He got a second mochila and filled it with worthless bits of torn paper. He placed that mochila over the real one, which was filled with mail and money. Sure enough, two outlaws stopped Cody and demanded his mochila. He threw the worthless mail bag at one of the outlaws, shot at the other one, and then trampled the first man with his horse. After that, he continued on his route, delivering the mail and money safely to the next station.[1]

One of the biggest dangers on the trail came from Native American attacks. More than two-thirds of the route ran across land inhabited by Native American tribes.[2] One of these tribes was the Paiute, who were unhappy with the increasing numbers of white settlers coming onto their land. The Paiute drove off horses from the stations and fired at riders as they passed through. The situation became even worse when some settlers—who were not connected with the Pony Express—committed violent acts against the Paiute.

On May 7, a party of Paiute warriors attacked Williams Station in Nevada. They killed the station keeper and several visitors and burned the station to the ground. Later, two station keepers at Egan Canyon were captured and almost killed by Paiute. They were only saved because a Pony Express rider alerted a nearby group of soldiers who rushed to the rescue.[3]

Because the Pony Express could not guarantee the safety of its riders and station keepers, the company made the difficult decision to shut down until conditions improved. From late May until late June, the mail piled up. Finally, after U.S. Army troops and bands of volunteer soldiers defeated the Paiute in battle, the short-lived Paiute War ended. However, riders still faced danger from Native Americans. During one of his runs, Haslam was attacked by a band of Paiute. One arrow broke his jaw and knocked out five teeth. He kept going. Episodes such as this only made the Pony Express riders seem more heroic and exciting.

The famous American writer Mark Twain traveled through the West and hoped to see a Pony Express rider in action. However, riders were easy to miss because they went by so quickly. "We heard only a whiz and a hail, and the swift phantom of the desert was gone before we could get our heads out of the windows,"[4] Twain wrote. Several days later, Twain finally got his chance. He explained:

> Away across the endless dead level of the prairie a black speck appears against the sky, and it is plain that it moves. . . . In a second it becomes a horse and rider, rising and falling . . . sweeping toward us nearer and nearer . . . and man and horse burst past our excited faces, and go winging away like a belated fragment of a storm![5]

Twain wrote about the Pony Express in his book *Roughing It* (published in 1872), increasing the legend of the Pony Express even more.

Samuel F.B. Morse is pictured with his telegraph in 1857. Morse's invention changed communication and meant the end of the Pony Express.

CHAPTER 5

The End of the Road

It had taken just over two months for Russell and his partners to put their dream into action. However, the Pony Express would shut down less than two years later with the click of a key. The reason for its end was simple. The telegraph came to the West.

The telegraph was invented by Samuel F. B. Morse in 1837. It used a system of electrical signals to send patterns of dots and dashes called Morse code along wires strung between tall poles. Each pattern stood for a different letter. Telegraph operators took down these messages and retyped them so they could be delivered. Now news could be sent between cities in hours instead of days.

The eastern and western parts of the United States had telegraph lines, but there was no connection through the middle of the United States. However, as more people settled in the west, the government decided to expand telegraph service. In June 1860, just two months after the Pony Express began its operations, the U.S. Congress authorized the building of a **transcontinental** telegraph line. Two crews began working to put up poles and wires. One crew moved east and the other moved west.

The need for quick communication became even more important when the Civil War broke out in April, 1861. Pony Express riders could watch workers building telegraph poles as they galloped over their routes in the summer of 1861.

The Pony Express had other troubles besides the telegraph. The COC&PP Express had spent $700,000 dollars to start and run the Pony Express. Within a year, the company was $200,000 in debt. Russell had hoped that the U.S. government would offer him a large contract to deliver the mail. That did not happen. Then Russell accepted a loan from a government official that turned out to be **illegal**. The Pony Express could not continue.

On October 24, 1861, the two telegraph construction crews met in Salt Lake City, Utah, and connected the wires. Two days later, newspapers

This painting captures the old and the new as a Pony Express rider passes workers laying telegraph poles across the West.

announced that the Pony Express had shut down. No one was surprised, but many people, especially in the West, were sad. The *Sacramento Bee* published this tribute: "Farewell, Pony. . . . Farewell and forever, thou staunch, wilderness-overcoming, swift-footed messenger."[1] California's *Pacific* magazine described the Pony Express's importance by saying, "A fast and faithful friend has the Pony been to our far-off state. Summer and winter, storm and shine, day and night, he has traveled like a weaver's shuttle back and forth till now his work is done. Good-bye Pony! You have served us well."[2]

Some riders were on the trail when the Pony Express shut down. They finished their routes so every piece of mail was delivered. The last mochila was turned in during November. Over the 18 months it existed, the Pony Express delivered 34,753 pieces of mail and covered more than 600,000 miles.[3] The riders lost just two mail shipments. The Pony Express only existed for a short time, but it truly changed America.

This statue in St. Joseph, Missouri, honors the riders of the Pony Express.

FACT OR FICTION?

The Pony Express was doomed from the start. It never made any money and drove its founders into **bankruptcy**. Also, since technology changes so fast, it was foolish to think that the Pony Express system would last forever. Just as mail delivery on horseback was faster than stagecoach, wagon trains, or ships, the telegraph made it much faster and easier to send messages over long distances.

Even though it only lasted 18 months, the Pony Express and its riders became an American legend and a symbol of America's spirit and determination. It must have been thrilling to see a Pony Express rider gallop through town at top speed, determined to get the mail through no matter what. The fact that Pony Express riders really did put their lives in danger every time they rode only added to the drama and romance.

The Pony Express became especially famous because of one of its riders. Years after riding for the Pony Express, William Cody—by then better known as Buffalo Bill—created a traveling production called the Wild West Show. The show was a huge success and traveled the country for many years. It featured different acts that dramatized Western adventure, such as sharpshooters, horseback riders, and Native Americans. Cody presented several of his Pony Express adventures in the show. His adventures were no doubt **exaggerated** to make them more exciting. These exaggerations became part of the Pony Express legend, even though they might not have been entirely true.

The Pony Express also became the subject of many books, paintings, and movies. Of course, these forms of media often take

This poster shows the excitement of Buffalo Bill Cody's Wild West Show, which featured riders on horseback and stories of dangerous adventures.

the truth and make it larger than life to make it more interesting. They create an image that people believe is true.

However, it is true that the Pony Express was an amazing and dangerous experience. Its riders faced death and performed heroic deeds in their dedication to getting the mail to its destination. The Pony Express also made it easier for people to settle in the West and still stay in touch with important news from back home. It united the country in a way that had not been possible before. For these reasons, the excitement and drama of the Pony Express are definitely fact.

A marker on Cody's grave in Golden, Colorado, honors his work with the Pony Express.

CHAPTER NOTES

Chapter 1: The Longest Ride

1. William Lightfoot Visscher, *A Thrilling and Truthful History of the Pony Express or Blazing the Westward Way* (Chicago: Charles T. Powner, 1946), p. 45.
2. Ibid.
3. Kathy Weiser, "Old West Legends: Pony Bob Haslam and the Longest Ride." Legends of America.com. http://www.legendsofamerica.com/we-ponybobhaslam.html
4. Ibid.

Chapter 2: The Need for Speed

1. Christopher Corbett, *Orphans Preferred: The Twisted Truth and Lasting Legend of the Pony Express* (New York: Broadway Books, 2003), p. 31.
2. Diane Yancey. *Life on the Pony Express* (San Diego, CA: Lucent Books, 2001), p. 12.
3. Ibid.
4. David Nevin, *The Expressmen* (New York: Time-Life Books, 1974), p. 33.
5. Arthur Chapman, *The Pony Express: The Record of a Romantic Adventure in Business* (New York: Cooper Square Publishers, 1971), p. 80.
6. Raymond W. and Mary Lund Settle, *Saddles and Spurs: The Pony Express Saga* (Lincoln, NE: University of Nebraska Press, 1955), p. 35.

Chapter 3: The First Ride

1. Roy S. Bloss, *Pony Express—The Great Gamble* (Berkeley, CA: Howell-North Press, 1959), p. 31.
2. Arthur E. Summerfield, *U.S. Mail: The Story of the United States Postal Service* (New York: Holt, Rinehart and Winston, 1960), p. 68.
3. Pony Express News (1860-1861). Pony Express Home Station.com. http://www.xphomestation.com/frm-news.html
4. Ibid.

Chapter 4: Danger on the Trail

1. William Lightfoot Visscher, *A Thrilling and Truthful History of the Pony Express, or Blazing the Westward Way* (Chicago: Charles T. Powner, 1946), p. 59.
2. Diane Yancey, *Life on the Pony Express* (San Diego, CA: Lucent Books, 2001), p. 77.
3. Roy S. Bloss, *Pony Express—The Great Gamble* (Berkeley, CA: Howell-North Press, 1959), p. 97.
4. Christopher Corbett, *Orphans Preferred: The Twisted Truth and Lasting Legend of the Pony Express* (New York: Broadway Books, 2003), p. 144.
5. Ibid.

Chapter 5: The End of the Road

1. Arthur E. Summerfield, *U.S. Mail: The Story of the United States Postal Service* (New York: Holt, Rinehart and Winston, 1960), p. 73.
2. Diane Yancey, *Life on the Pony Express* (San Diego, CA: Lucent Books, 2001), p. 93.
3. Simone Payment, *The Pony Express: A Primary Source History of the Race to Bring Mail to the American West* (New York: Rosen Publishing Company, 2005), p. 52.

bankruptcy (BANK-rupt-see)—unable to pay money owed to others

contract (KON-trakt)—a legal agreement between people or companies

enterprise (EN-tur-prize)—an important project, especially one facing difficulties

exaggerated (eg-ZAJ-uh-ray-ted)—made something seem bigger or more important than it really was

home stations (HOME STAY-shuhnz)—buildings on the Pony Express route where riders could get a meal and rest

illegal (ih-LEE-guhl)—against the law

outlaws (OUT-lawz)—people who break the law

relay station (REE-lay STAY-shuhn)—a building on the Pony Express route where riders could change horses

stagecoaches (STAGE-koh-chez)—wagons pulled by horses and used to carry passengers or mail over long distances

station keeper (STAY-shuhn KEE-per)—a man who ran a Pony Express station

superintendent (soo-per-in-TEN-duhnt)—a person in charge of an organization

telegrams (TEL-uh-gramz)—messages sent by telegraph

telegraph (TEL-uh-graf)—a system for sending messages by wire over long distances, using a code of electrical signals

territory (TER-uh-tor-ee)—land controlled by the United States that has not become a state

transcontinental (tranz-kon-tuh-NEN-tuhl)—across a continent

Bloss, Roy S. *Pony Express—The Great Gamble*. Berkeley, CA: Howell-North Press, 1959.

Chapman, Arthur. *The Pony Express: The Record of a Romantic Adventure in Business*. New York: Cooper Square Publishers, 1971.

Corbett, Christopher. *Orphans Preferred: The Twisted Truth and Lasting Legend of the Pony Express*. New York: Broadway Books, 2003.

Corbett, Christopher and Russell Alan Spreeman. "Pony Bob Haslam." Cowboys and Indians.com. http://www.cowboysindians.com/Cowboys-Indians/October-2011/Pony-Bob-Haslan/

Nevin, David. *The Expressmen*. New York: Time-Life Books, 1974.

Payment, Simone. *The Pony Express: A Primary Source History of the Race to Bring Mail to the American West*. New York: Rosen, 2005.

Pony Express News (1860-1861). Pony Express Home Station.com. http://www.xphomestation.com/frm-news.html

Settle, Raymond W. and Mary Lund Settle. *Saddles and Spurs: The Pony Express Saga*. Lincoln, NE: University of Nebraska Press, 1955.

Summerfield, Arthur E. *U.S. Mail: The Story of the United States Postal Service*. New York: Holt, Rinehart and Winston, 1960.

Visscher, William Lightfoot. *A Thrilling and Truthful History of the Pony Express or Blazing the Westward Way*. Chicago: Charles T. Powner, 1946.

Weiser, Kathy. "Old West Legends: Pony Bob Haslam and the Longest Ride." Legends of America.com. http://www.legendsofamerica.com/we-ponybobhaslam.html

Yancey, Diane. *Life on the Pony Express*. San Diego, CA: Lucent Books, 2001.

Hall, Margaret. *The Pony Express*. Vero Beach, FL: Rourke, 2010.

Kay, Verla. *Whatever Happened to the Pony Express?* New York: Penguin, 2010.

McNeese, Tim. *The Pony Express: Bringing Mail to the American West*. New York: Chelsea House, 2009.

Ratliff, Tom. *You Wouldn't Want to Be a Pony Express Rider!* New York: Franklin Watts, 2012.

Savage, Jeff. *Daring Pony Express Riders*. Berkeley Heights, NJ: Enslow Publishers, Inc., 2012.

Spradlin, Michael P. *Off Like the Wind! The First Ride of the Pony Express*. New York: Walker & Company, 2010.

ON THE INTERNET

Pony Express
http://www.42explore2.com/pony.htm

The Pony Express
http://www.socialstudiesforkids.com/articles/ushistory/ponyexpress.htm

The Pony Express National Historic Trail
http://www.nps.gov/poex

The Pony Express National Museum
http://www.ponyexpress.org/history

Westward Expansion: The Pony Express
http://www.ducksters.com/history/westward_expansion/pony_express.php

PHOTO CREDITS: All design elements from Thinkstock/Sharon Beck; Cover, pp. 1, 27—Library of Congress; p. 4—Public domain; p. 6—Famartin/cc by-sa 4.0; pp. 8-9—William Henry Jackson/Public domain; p. 10—Smithsonian National Postal Nuseum, Pony Express/Public domain; pp. 13, 14—U.S. National Archives & Records Administration/Public domain; p. 18—Sarony/Public domain; p. 22—Mathew Brady/Public domain; p. 24—North Wind Picture Archives/Alamy Stock Photo; p. 25—cc by-sa 2.5.

ABOUT THE AUTHOR

Joanne Mattern is the author of many books for children on a variety of subjects, including history and biography. She has written many biographies for Mitchell Lane. Joanne loves to learn about people, places, and events and bring historical figures to life for today's readers. She lives in New York State with her husband, children, and several pets.